Hoppy Passover!

Linda Glaser   Illustrated by Daniel Howarth

www.av2books.com

Go to **www.av2books.com**, and enter this book's unique code.

BOOK CODE

P234108

AV² by Weigl brings you media enhanced books that support active learning.

First Published by

ALBERT WHITMAN & COMPANY
Publishing children's books since 1919

Your **AV² Media Enhanced** book gives you a fiction readalong online. Log on to **www.av2books.com** and enter the unique book code from this page to use your readalong.

AV² Readalong Navigation

HIGHLIGHTED TEXT

HOME 🏠

All children like to play.
They dig in the dirt,
they splash in water.
They build roads and bridges
for their cars and trucks.
They play games
like hide-and-go-seek.
Children love to just run.
What do you like to play!

20   21

CLOSE ⊗

START READING

READ

TITLE INFORMATION

INFO

AV² READALONG   BACK READ NEXT   INFO

PAGE TURNING

BACK NEXT

PAGE PREVIEW

Published by AV² by Weigl
350 5th Avenue, 59th Floor New York, NY 10118
Websites: www.av2books.com   www.weigl.com

Library of Congress Control Number: 2014937157

ISBN 978-1-4896-2822-0 (hardcover)
ISBN 978-1-4896-2823-7 (single user eBook)
ISBN 978-1-4896-2824-4 (multi-user eBook)

Printed in the United States of America in North Mankato, Minnesota
1 2 3 4 5 6 7 8 9 0 18 17 16 15 14

042014
WEP080414

Text copyright ©2011 by Linda Glaser.
Illustrations copyright ©2011 by Daniel Howarth.
Published in 2011 by Albert Whitman & Company.

What's that funny dish, Grandma?" asked Violet.

"It's the Seder plate for Passover," said Grandma.

"Remember the special meal we had here last year?"

"No." Violet and Simon shook their heads. "Can we do it again?"

"Of course!" said Grandma.

"I want to help." Violet hopped up and down.
"Me, too!" Simon hopped so hard his ears flip-flopped.

4

"Here." Mama handed them books. "You can set out the Haggadahs."
"Ooh! A story!" exclaimed Violet.
"Yes," said Papa. "From long ago, when Jews were slaves in Egypt."

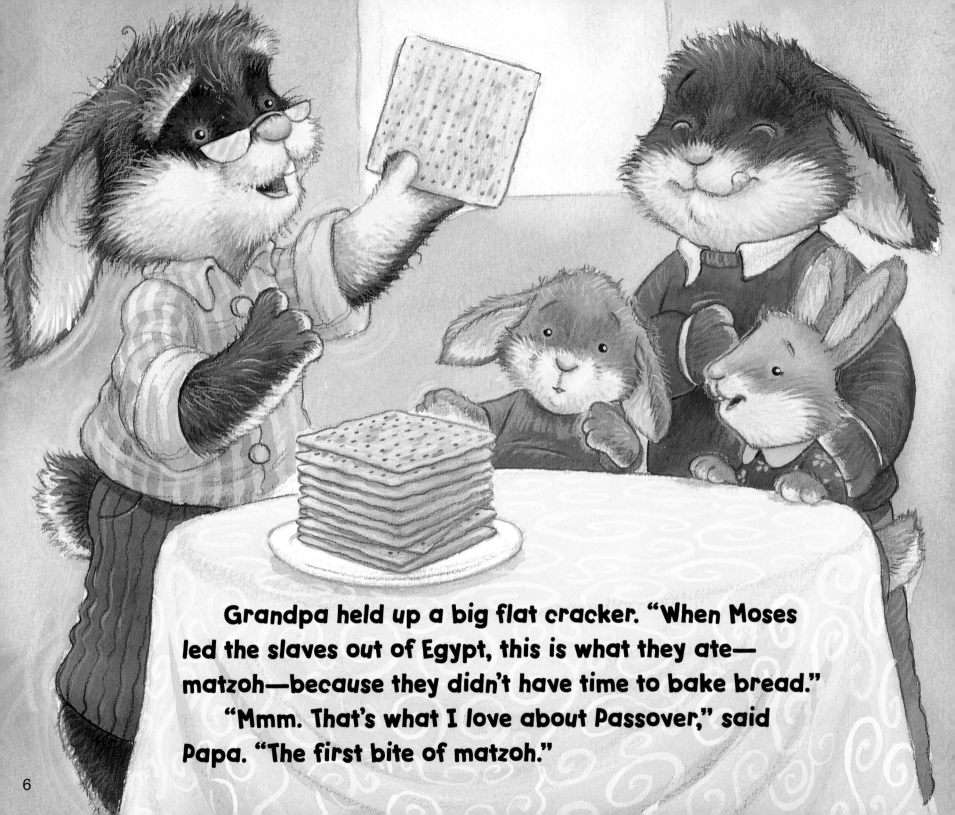

Grandpa held up a big flat cracker. "When Moses led the slaves out of Egypt, this is what they ate—matzoh—because they didn't have time to bake bread."

"Mmm. That's what I love about Passover," said Papa. "The first bite of matzoh."

6

"I want a taste!" said Violet.
"Me, too!" said Simon.
"Very soon," said Papa.
"We'll wait for the Seder."

Grandma gave Simon
a bunch of parsley.
"Please put this on the
Seder plate."

8

"Mmm." Simon munched. "This is what I love about Passover!"

Soon . . . oops! he ate the whole bunch. Grandma laughed. "Here's more for you and the plate."

"I just made charoset," said Grandma. "See? It looks like clay that the slaves made into bricks. But it doesn't taste like bricks." She smiled. "Try some."

Violet nibbled and nibbled. "Mmm. This is what I love about Passover. More bricks, please." She giggled.

Mama set a roasted egg, a bone,
and a horseradish root on the Seder plate.
Violet and Simon did not try *any* of those!

Grandpa handed them a stack of pillows. "One for each chair," he said.

"You know why?" asked Papa. "The slaves weren't allowed to rest on pillows."

Grandpa nodded. "But now we do because we're free."

Violet and Simon tried out every pillow. Bounce, bounce, bounce. "We're free!" they sang out. And their ears flew. Wheeee!

Everyone sat down. The grownups read from the Haggadah.
Violet and Simon drank grape juice and dipped parsley in salt water.

"Now watch closely," said Grandpa. He broke a piece of matzoh and wrapped some in a napkin. "I'm going to hide this, and you'll look for it later." He hopped around the room grinning.

Violet and Simon watched closely. But where did it go? They didn't know.

"Why is this night different from all other nights?"

Next, Papa helped them say the Four Questions. Then Violet and Simon ate matzoh. It was dry and crunchy.

They even tasted a tiny bit of horseradish. It made them shiver from nose to toes.

They quickly ate *lots* of charoset. Violet licked her lips. "More bricks, please!"

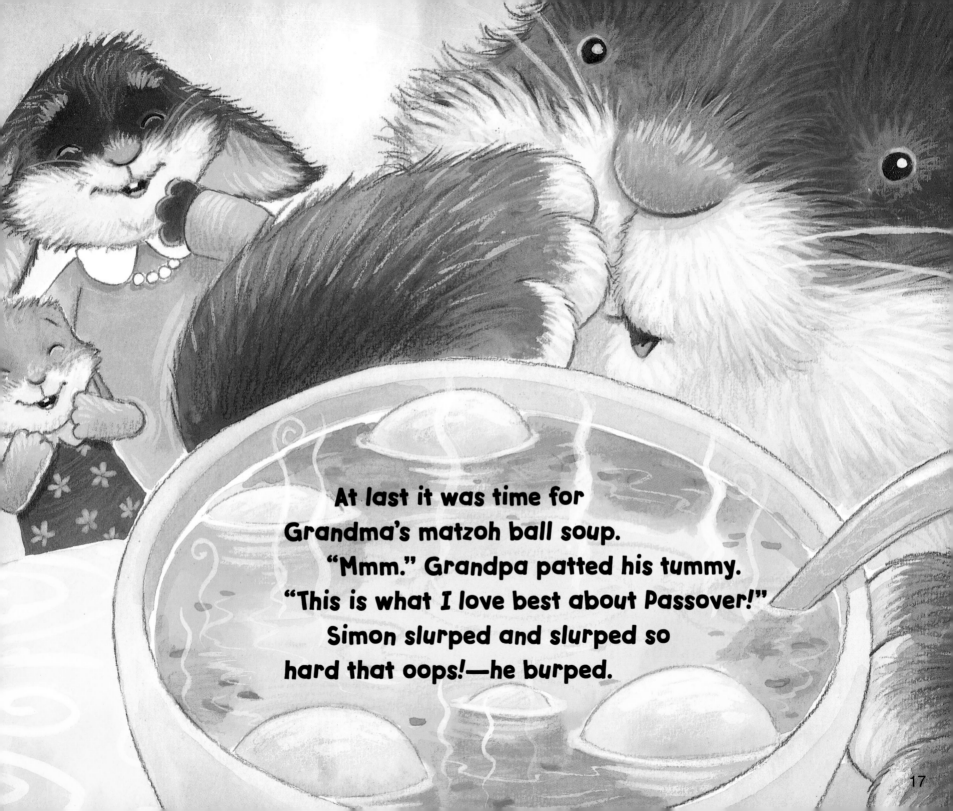

At last it was time for
Grandma's matzoh ball soup.
"Mmm." Grandpa patted his tummy.
"This is what *I* love best about Passover!"
Simon slurped and slurped so
hard that oops!—he burped.

17

After dinner Papa
said, "It's time to find
the afikomen—the
hidden matzoh."
Violet and Simon
searched everywhere.

"Ooh, look!" Violet laughed.
"I see it! I see it!" Simon giggled so hard his tummy jiggled.

Grandpa gave them each a present for finding the matzoh—
a new picture book!

They hopped around the room. Hop. Hop. Hop.

Grandma beamed. "Happy Passover!"

Grandpa shook his head. "Around here, it's
Hoppy Passover!"

"Now hop over and open the door for the prophet Elijah," said Grandpa.

"I don't see him," called Simon.

"That's OK. Nobody does," explained Grandpa. "Watch his cup. See if he drinks any wine."

They watched and watched.

"I think he did," whispered Violet.

"Me, too," whispered Simon.

"A tiny sip."

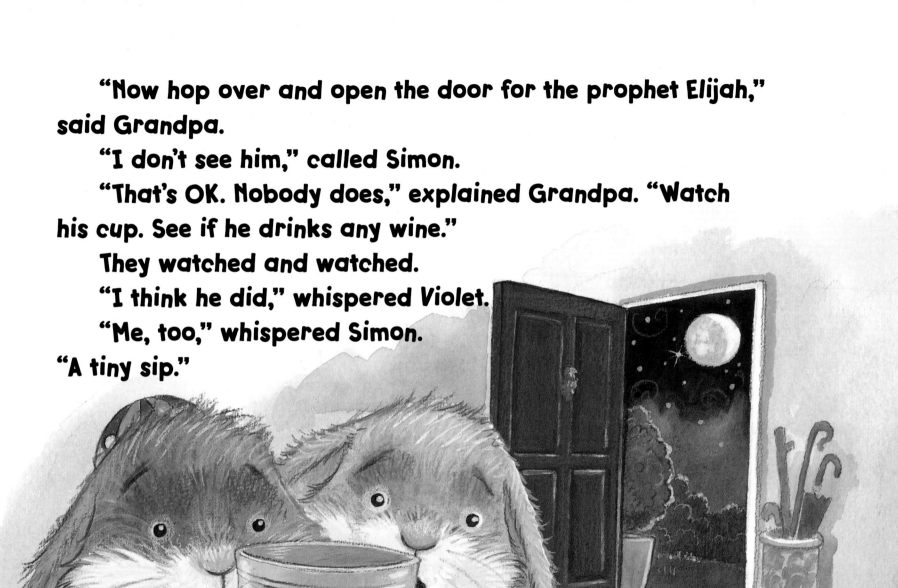

"Chad gadya, chad gadya . . . "

Finally they all sang songs.
Mama beamed. "This is what I love best."
Papa nodded. "Passover reminds us how good life is."

"It sure does," said Grandpa.
"You know what I love best about Passover?" asked Grandma.
Violet and Simon shook their heads. "What?"

Grandma wrapped her arms around both of them. "YOU!"